P9-CRO-473

For my parents (and
Sonia Jones) ~ G.D.

For all my family,
with love ~ M.T.

tiger tales
5 River Road, Suite 128, Wilton, CT 06897
Published in the United States 2021
Originally published in Great Britain 2021
by Little Tiger Press Ltd.
Text by Georgiana Deutsch
Text copyright © 2021 Little Tiger Press Ltd.
Illustrations copyright © 2021 Megan Tadden
ISBN-13: 978-1-68010-233-8
ISBN-10: 1-68010-233-8
Printed in China
LTP/2800/3509/1020
All rights reserved
2 4 6 8 10 9 7 5 3 1

www.tigertalesbooks.com

Looking for Sleep

by Georgiana Deutsch

Illustrated by Megan Tadden

tiger tales

It was bedtime in the forest,
but Wolf was wide awake.
He just couldn't sleep!

Wolf tried a
warm bath

and a tasty
bedtime snack.

He even hung
upside down.
But would sleep come?
Not a chance!

It was very strange.
"Sleep must be hiding," Wolf
declared. "I'll just have to go
and find it!" And off he went.

Wolf peered into
a dark den.
"SLEEEEP!
Are you in here?"
he hollered.

Sleep didn't answer,
but Badger did!
"Wolf!" he grumped.
"You interrupted
my dream!"

"I'm sorry," Wolf said. "I'm looking for sleep! And if you were dreaming, that means it's only a whisker away!"

Badger huffed. "Well, we'd better go and find it. But no more shouting!"

Wolf and Badger hadn't gone far
when they heard a lullaby.
There, singing softly under the
stars, was Hedgehog.
"Sleep is never far from a
lullaby!" whispered Wolf.
"I'll creep over and
catch it!"

"Quickly!" grumbled
Badger. "And be QUIET!"
Wolf tiptoed closer
and closer, until . . .

...CRACK!
went a twig.
"EEK!" yelped Hedgehog.

"Don't be scared!" said Wolf.
"We're just looking for sleep!
Is it here with you?"

Hedgehog shook her quills.
"Maybe it's hiding nearby!"
she squeaked.

The friends
searched everywhere,
from the woods . . .

to the shores of
the moonlit lake.
"I'm exhausted!"
grumbled Badger,
and he gave a huge . . .

YAWN!

"Badger—don't move!"
cried Wolf. "Sleep
loves hiding in yawns!"
"In YAWNS?!"
growled Badger.
"That's the silliest
thing I've ever heard!"

"Why don't we ask Owl?" Hedgehog said. "I bet she'll know where sleep is hiding!"

But as they got closer to Owl's
tree, they heard a terrible noise.
"What's that?" gulped Wolf.
"A monster?!" squeaked Hedgehog.

"It's just Rabbit snoring," sighed Badger.

But this gave Wolf a great idea. "I bet sleep is hiding in Rabbit's nose," he whispered. "I just need to tickle it out!"

Wolf found a feather, and . . .

SNUFFLE-SNUFFLE . . .

SNORT . . .

What a ruckus! And STILL
sleep was nowhere to be found.
Wolf had had ENOUGH!

"OWL!" he howled. "We can't
find sleep ANYWHERE!"

Owl peered down from her moonlit branch. "What's all this talk about looking for sleep?" she chuckled. "I'm not sure you'll ever find it . . . ."

"NEVER find sleep?!"
gasped Wolf.
"What will we DO?!"
cried Hedgehog.
Badger stamped his foot.
"This is Wolf's fault for
scaring it off!" he sulked.

But Owl just smiled kindly. "Sleep will find YOU," she told them, "but only when you're tired and still, and feeling safe. Like when you're listening to a bedtime story."

Wolf thought hard. "Owl?" he blinked.
"Could you maybe tell us a story?"
"Absolutely!" beamed Owl.

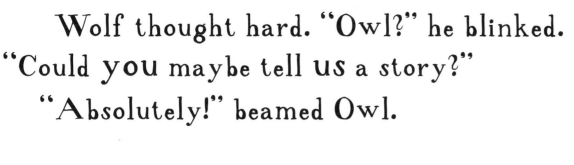

The friends snuggled up
under the twinkling stars
while Owl found the
perfect tale.

"It was bedtime in the forest," she began, "but Wolf was wide awake. Tonight, sleep was hiding in the COZIEST place of all . . ."

...in the whispered words
of a bedtime story."

31192022111171